WELCOME TO DINSMORE
THE WORLD'S GREATEST STORE

WELCOME TO DINSMORE
THE WORLD'S GREATEST STORE

by William Boniface

Illustrated by Tom Kerr

Andrews and McMeel
A Universal Press Syndicate Company
Kansas City

This book is for
The Li'l Buckaroo, that's who!

W.B.

Designed by Barrie Maguire
ISBN: 0-8362-0743-2

Library of Congress Catalog Card Number: 95-76484

Attention: Schools and Businesses
Andrews and McMeel books are available at quantity discounts with bulk
purchase for educational, business, or sales promotional use. For informa-
tion, please write to: Special Sales Department, Andrews and McMeel, 4900
Main Street, Kansas City, Missouri 64112.

Welcome to Dinsmore,

the world's greatest store!

Whatever you search for, we've got it, and more.

So what brings you here in this cold, rainy mess?

No, wait, now, don't tell me, I'll bet I can guess!

You need something badly. It shows in your face.

So follow me in, and I'll show you the place.

There's no need to drip when you come through our door,

Because of the hot air that blows from the floor.

It comes from a Blowhard, which, as you can see,

Produces the hottest air west of D.C.

But don't stand there long, or you'll no sooner find,

You're caught in an updraft and left far behind.

And past the main entrance you'll find quite a sight.

A sixteen-piece orchestra, brassy and bright.

With four violinists, three cellos, two flutes,

And two men with saws wearing lumberjack suits,

One trumpet, one tuba, one long slide trombone,

And a crusty old man on a wood xylophone.

And the world's fattest lady who plucks at a harp,

As they play "Shopper's Waltz," by Strauss, in D-sharp.

But don't listen long, there's so much to be seen,

From one up to nine, and the floors in between.

You've something to find, so let's see what we've got.

Don't speak up just yet, though. We've got quite a lot.

Our buyers at Dinsmore went out of their way,

To search the world over by night and by day,

And wow you with goods of an awesome array.

Perhaps what you'd like is a bit of perfume,

Step up to the counter, there's plenty of room.

We've fragrances formerly lost to the past,

Like the eau de cologne of King Louis the Last.

And others most people thought never could be,

Like Circe's sixth scent, which she stole from the sea.

These, and far more, were sniffed out by our buyer,

Which shows why at Dinsmore we hold our nose higher.

Whether countess or clown you can't make an impression,

Without stopping by our cosmetics concession.

The counter is run by three very old sisters,

Whose fingers (though covered with sores and with blisters),

Work wonders with makeup that all will enjoy,

As they claim that they once did for Helen of Troy.

And as experts in makeup, their praises I'll sing,

But to use some themselves wouldn't be a bad thing.

9585HC

It's time to move on, though, just look at a clock,

And Dinsmore has got the most clocks on the block.

We've clocks that run sideways and forwards and back,

And alarm clocks that wake you up out of the sack.

In all there's exactly ten thousand and nine,

In sizes that range from Big Ben to a Tine.

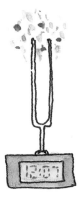

The hourglass Tine is so small and so fine,

That it sifts neon atoms like sand through its spine.

I can't see it myself, but I'm told it's divine.

The rugs on our second floor aren't what you think.

These carpets can fly, and it tickles me pink.

There's no other place you can buy flying carpets,

Our private importer has cornered the market.

He's Sheik Ali Akbar el Hasan Ben Sued,

And he's one highly capable Bedouin dude.

Where it is that he finds them I don't have a clue.

And how we found him is a mystery too!

And if you want furniture brought to your door,

Our delivery birds won't regard it a chore.

One is named Charlie, the other one's Zane.

And each is the size of a jumbo jet plane.

In spite of their bulk they're both graceful and agile,

And won't damage objects no matter how fragile.

So, for Tiffany lamps, or pianos from Steinway,

Transported to you in a stylish and fine way,

Aerially speaking there's no one that's better,

Than Dinsmore, of course, and our friends of a feather.

All this talk makes one hungry, but as you can see,

The Dinsmore Café is our next stop on three.

We'll have a quick snack while we put up our feets,

And relax in our patented Fuzzy-Butt Seats.

Massaging your footsies and toes while you eat,

They make dining relaxing and shopping a treat.

For lunch, now, of course, you can make your own choice.
Just speak to your menu. It transfers your voice,
To the head Dinsmore chef, who's at work in the rear.
Be sure to speak loudly! Make sure he can hear!
Who wants to get stuck with an order of muck,
When what you requested was candy-glazed duck.
While muck is nutritious, it's just not the same,
And it won't satisfy when you've duck on the brain.

Then wash it all down with a juice we call codberry.

That's made from a scarce and unusually odd berry.

It grows in the depths of the trench Marianas,

To get there is easy, (I'll be very honest).

The tough part is picking them out of the snouts,

Of the over-sized trouts where the codberry sprouts.

Why they sprout in the snout of a trout I'm in doubt,

But the divers at Dinsmore have gotten some out,

And brought us a drink that we're happy to tout.

For dessert, now I think we should try something new.

It's a tasty and rare dish that comes from Peru.

High up in the Andes there live some poor llamas.

They're all pretty cold, but it's worse for the mamas.

They give ice cream instead of the milk one expects,

And it's made every one of them broken down wrecks.

The ice cream, however, is out of this world.

My favorite is key lime and wintergreen swirled.

And the llamas will one day be over their traumas.

They're saving their profits to buy the Bahamas.

A meal like that could make anyone tired,

So I have a thought that I think is inspired.

We'll take a brief snooze when we reach the fourth floor.

It's Bedding and Linens, but try not to snore.

We've beds that sleep one, two or three, five or eight,

Like this one belonging to Catherine the Great.

Lie back for a moment and let your head rest.

The pillows at Dinsmore are simply the best.

They're stuffed with the feathers
that come from a bird,
Which molts once a year
every April the third.
These feathers (so light
that no measure's been found),
Take nearly ten months
to descend to the ground.
With feathers that light
from a bird that's so small,
It's a wonder we've got any
pillows at all.
But the men Dinsmore
hires are patient you see,
And brave, I might add,
to stand under that tree.

APRIL

Now is snoozing a way
to find out what you want?
I think that it isn't!
So on with our jaunt.
The ladies' department
is next up on five.
Don't look so disgusted!
I'm sure you'll survive.

A purse for your mother might be what you need.

I know one I think that she'd like. Yes, indeed!

It came to us straight from the island of Crete.

It's Pandora's purse, and it's really quite neat.

It's a bottomless bag that will never get full.

It can hold as much change as a cargo ship's hull.

Not to mention a truckload of lipsticks and keys,

And a mountain of mints, and a circus of fleas.

Despite all it holds it weighs less than a pup,

So even your mother can't fill the thing up.

If that's not enough to make Mom flip her wig,

Then stop by our wig shop and see something big.

Our wigs are all bought from the country of Quigg.

Where wigs sprout on trees just like sprigs on a twig.

And everyone wears them including each pig.

The sprig from each twig's an original wig.

But Quigg has more wigs than they've people or pigs,

So the bigwig of Quigg, to get out of this gig,

Sold off all the extras to Dinsmore, you dig?

TAKE IT FOR A TEST DRIVE

Perhaps what you search for
is something for Dad.
We've things on the sixth floor
that aren't half bad.
Our most popular item's
the Dad-i-o-matic,
An easy chair built for
the TV fanatic.
During football most fathers
are likely to cheer,
When at halftime it serves up
a pizza and beer.
It also trims nose hairs
and gives him a shave,
Picks lint from his navel,
and, if he feels brave,
It gives him one heckuva
permanent wave.
To get one would leave
any father ecstatic,
And Dinsmore's the place
for the Dad-i-o-matic.

We've come a long way,
but it's not far enough.
Is there nothing you search for
amidst all that stuff?
The seventh floor's next,
and it's worth a quick look,
In case what you want is
a song or a book.

We've all of the music you ever could want.

Including a singer we're quite proud to flaunt.

He's Carmichael Cradock, the Cricket Caruso.

Most crickets can't sing, yet he's able to do so.

Discovered by Dinsmore last summer in Spain,

We've made him a star from Hawaii to Maine.

He's currently touring and wowing the nation,

The ultimate two-inch high, six-leg sensation.

So stop by and see why he's topping the charts.

And chirping his way into all of our hearts.

Or stop in the bookshop and see what's on top,

Our pop-up selection is cream of the crop.

We gave some old authors a brand-new dimension,

And heftier prices I'd rather not mention.

Pinocchio's nose grows right off of the page.

Our Heidi, with Alps, has become quite the rage.

The Jack in our books is more nimble and sprier,

Our Dante's *Inferno* has flames that leap higher.

Or look in our *Roget's* for words meaning great,

And Dinsmore's the one that pops up on your plate.

Our sporting goods area spans the eighth floor,

And is home to the Great Dinsmore Balancing Corps.

They balance on footballs and golf balls on tees,

And baseballs and beachballs and cross-country skis.

One stands on tennis balls. Talk about nerve!

While someone below tries to practice his serve.

And they don't stop when finished, despite how it looks.

They go back to Accounting and balance our books.

know what you want, though. I've known from the start,
The ninth floor would hold something dear to your heart.
We formed a joint venture with Santa Claus, Inc.,
(with approval of Elves Local 7, I think).
And brought the North Pole to Dinsmore's top floor,
To transform it into a toy store galore.

And these Elves are as clever
as clever can be,
The toys they create
are quite something to see.

Like edible Easy-Shape
Gelatin Goo,
That lets you mold objects
you eat when you're through.

Or jet-propelled bicycles,
skateboards, and trikes,
Or Velcro pajamas
for rambunctious tykes.

And dolls that not only
speak Russian and Latin,
They study high fashion
in midtown Manhattan.

Da
Da

But my favorite toy
is the Peddle-O-Copter.
They've tried and they've tried
but they just haven't topped 'er.

And toys that we sell must be top of the line,

So here's where we make sure they're working just fine.

Our steam locomotives must all locomote.

We test in a moat that our boats can all float.

The trampolines must have a bounce in their springs,

And all of our Pong balls have got to have Pings.

If punching bags punch back, they're just not allowed,

While every stuffed lion has got to be proud.

And every toy soldier is put through this drill,

So every toy sold here will give kids a thrill.

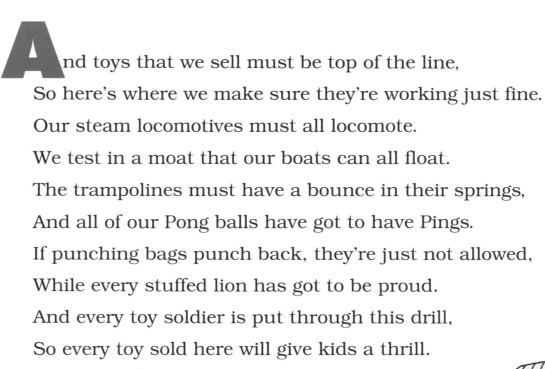

You've seen the whole store, now, from bottom to top.

Whatever you're seeking we've got in our shop.

So speak up my boy, tell me what brought you here.

Or whisper it to me. I'll lend you my ear.

Uh, huh, . . .

Oh, my goodness! . . .

I now see the rush.

To the left,

down that aisle . . .

. . . and remember to flush!